THE CHRONICLES

OF

ODYXENIA

THE AURORAN

ONSLAUGHT

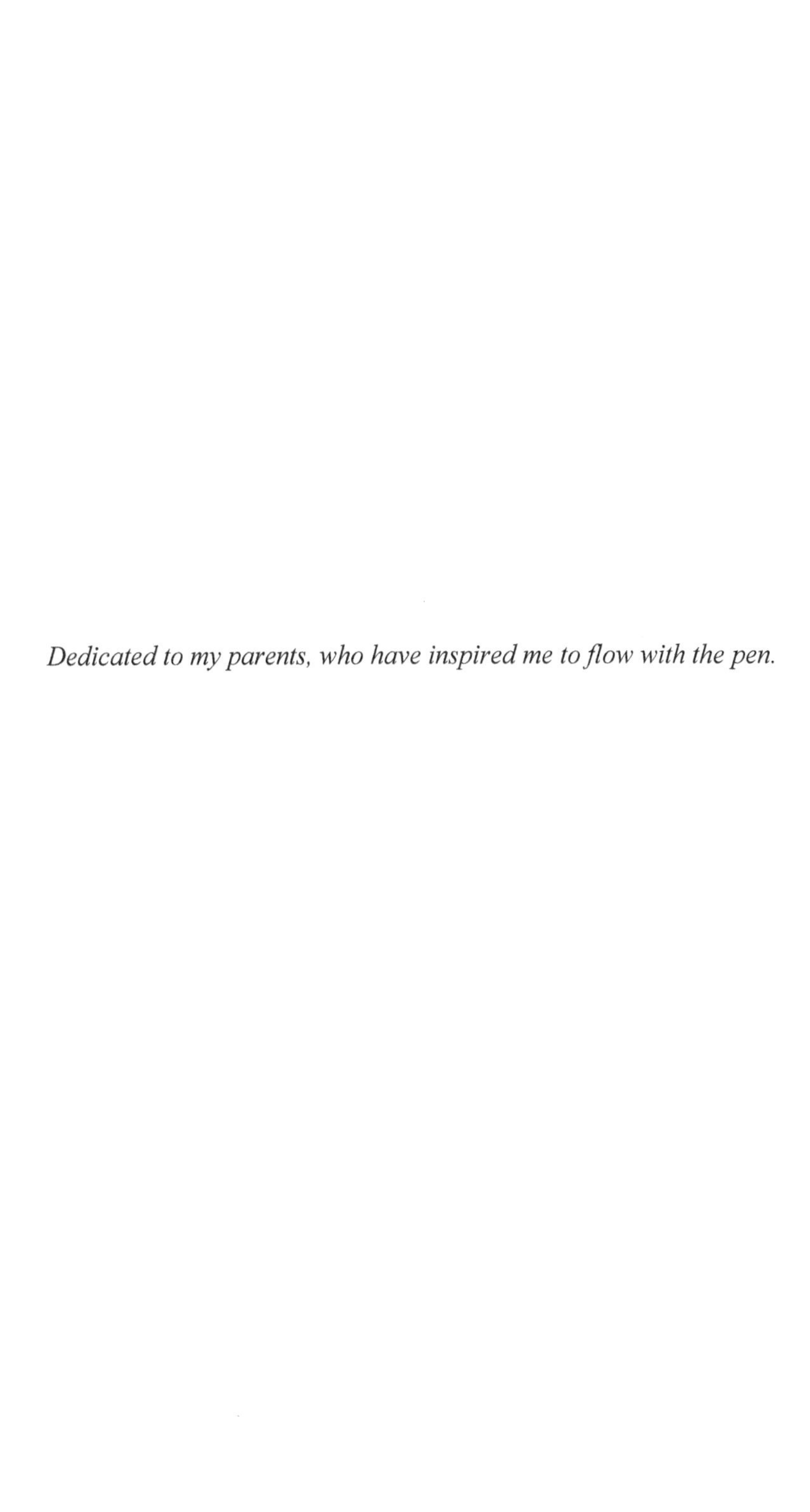

Dedicated to my parents, who have inspired me to flow with the pen.

CONTENTS

Acknowledgements

This section acknowledges all those who have assisted in the making and production of this book.

Firstly, I would like to thank my parents who have helped me develop my passion for writing because of which this book is written.

Next, my teachers, Ms. Aratrika and Ms. Vinita for assisting me in improving my language proficiency.

Lastly, I would like to thank Notion Press for the wonderful platform I have been provided with for writing, formatting, editing and publishing this book.

MAP OF

ODYXENIA

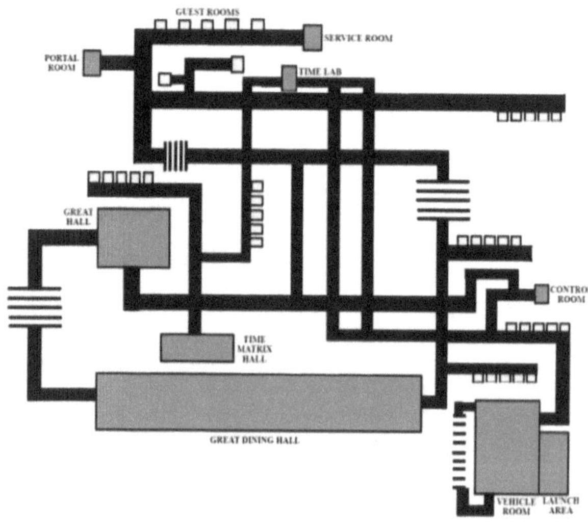

I

The Party

Edward

Banners went up, so did cries of joy. The celebrations were very intense. The victory of the five Odyxi was all that mattered.

Edward was, however, grumpy. He and his companions Sam Brer, Peter Brer, Jack Olan Tern and John Diss had gone through a rather unusual (and equally annoying) transition in their lives the previous day – so would anyone else if they'd been peacefully playing a game of tag, uneventfully yanked into a swirling portal, realizing they weren't the only people there, going on a dangerous journey to defeat a Giant and his armada commanders...Yes, life was normal. Now the entire group of portal-people (who called themselves Odyxi, members of the Time Base of Odyxenia) were rejoicing *their* victory, and Edward found it unfair that he and his friends were the ones whose lives had been put on the line that very day.

The entire group paraded to the Great Dining Hall. Tables blanketed in white, gold stripes lining them were adorned with hundreds of plates, cups and what not. An ocean of varieties occupied the place, and everyone ate loads.

'Welcome back, heroes of Odyxenia,' Solseter, the Son of Odyxen, the God of Time, addressed the victorious Odyxi.

'We'd like to hear from you. Tell us more about your magnificent adventures! Edward? You first.'

Edward Toast stood up. He cleared his throat.

'*Hem, hem,*' he hem-hemmed. 'Alright. First of all, I hope you meant sarcasm, Solseter.' He drew imaginary quotation marks with his fingers in the air.

'So,' he began. 'I recount my tale. So first, I opened the door into a misty landscape, which I felt my way out of. Then, I took a coaster to the mountaintop. There, I killed this giant and took the Jewel. I came down and went through a door. And I was back. I didn't get hurt at all guys. Easiest journey ever. Giant was a piece of cake, really –'

'Ok, ok,' said Solseter uncertainly. 'That was truly amazing. Jack, would you like to speak up?'

'Si, *señor,*' Jack said.

Jack, John, Sam and Peter shared similar views about their 'magnificent' adventures.

'Fascinating, Peter,' said he after Peter Brer had finished sharing his emotional dilemma about murdering the Spider Queen Arachnis and a dragon, and being reassured that her sister Arachania would take over the rule of the arthropods.

'Wait a sec,' Edward interrupted. 'Where the flip is Anne?' Looking around, everyone suddenly realized Anne, the brainiac and unofficial leader of the entire flock of time warriors wasn't there. A lot of murmuring broke out. Solseter shushed them.

'She's at the Time Lab, working on –' He stopped himself.

Edward stood up. 'On what?' he asked. 'You'll see,' the old man said. 'Now, three cheers for the champions, once again!' he cried. An amazingly loud applause accompanied them. Edward felt annoyed that Solseter had changed the subject.

Before he could bring it back, Solseter got up. 'Alright, everyone off to bed,' he ushered them to their rooms. 'Already?' asked Sam, clearly expectant for more time to party. 'Nope. You're off to bed. Tomorrow morning, I need to introduce you guys to this base. You've got a lot to learn if you want to become proper Odyxi.'

'So what are we now, sacrificial pre-teens?'

'Edward, please go to bed.'

'I hate it when you change the subject.'

'I'd *love* it if you'd go to bed, like, *right now*.'

Not wanting to make the Time God's Son angry, Edward decided to stop protesting (resentfully, of course) and get some rest. The thought made him sleepy, and, well, annoyed.

'Boy would I like to hear some Odyxenian Mythology,' Edward said to Sam sarcastically, rolling his eyes. He immediately regretted it – Solseter, being Odyxen's Son, looked offended. 'Sorry,' he said sheepishly.

'Well, goodnight.'

'What now?' Edward asked, as he accompanied his friends to the rooms.

'Guess we wait and find out,' Sam said. 'G'night, guys.'

As Edward entered his room, he felt a multitude of emotions sweep over him: Bitterness, anger and resentfulness (no prizes for guessing who these were directed to). However, he felt a sort of...*good* feeling too – a victorious, triumphant sort of feeling. He thought about how much had changed about his life that day. He lay in bed and began replaying the entire day in his head. But before he knew it, he became drowsy, and his body shut down.

II

The Midnight Call

NEE-NAW! NEE-NAW! NEE-NAW!

Edward, on hearing the alarm, leapt out of bed and crashed headfirst into a wall. Clutching his sore head in his weary arms, he felt his way to the light switch and pressed his thumb on it. The lights flickered on. Why, oh *why* would he never get good sleep?

A furious Edward then slammed his palm on the OFF switch next to the alarm speaker. 'The hell,' he said. 'What's going on?' Hearing alarms stop in the rooms next to his, Edward knew his friends were awake. He wearily unlocked his door and stepped outside.

Instantly, motion sensors on the floor activated the hallway lights. *Click, click, click* went the other room doors as a sleepy Sam, jumpy Jack, jabbering John and pestered Peter stepped out their rooms. Suddenly, there was a *thud* as the loudspeaker came alive. It was, unmistakably, the voice of Anne Ayon.

'*Attention, Odyxi. Emergency, please report to the Control Room ASAP.*' With another loud *thud*, the announcement ended. 'Guys,' Edward said. 'Let's stick together. If we're making it out of the labyrinth within a couple of days, we should be fine.'

'Erm, sure, Ed,' Sam stammered. The others murmured in agreement.

'Alright, then. Let's proceed.'

They walked, and they walked, and they walked, and they walked. They read many labels on doors: PORTAL ROOM, SERVICE ROOM (!), VEHICLE ROOM (?) and many more. They even made it to the Great Hall and the Dining Hall. But no CONTROL ROOM anywhere. They ran in circles, literally, not knowing what to do.

'Aw, man,' said John. 'We're lost, aren't we?'

'I hate to admit it,' Jack remarked, 'but I think we are.'

'Don't waste your energy. We're not making any progress. We ought to wait for someone to rescue us,' Sam advised.

And so they did. They waited for what seemed like ages, when the loudspeaker blared again: '*Mr. Toast, Mr. Diss, Mr. Tern, Mr. Brer and Mr. other*

Brer, please report to the Control Room now.' They recognized the voice – it wasn't Anne this time, instead, it was Elsa Vador.

As the loudspeaker gave a *thud*, another voice was heard. This time, it was not from the loudspeaker. 'HELLO!' It was shrill and strict. 'Anne!' they yelled together. Jack began. '*M'aidez*! SOS! Help! Save us! Dot-dot-'

'Oh, shut up, Jack,' Edward said.

'Not helping,' John groaned.

Just then, they heard footsteps running towards them from behind. They spun around as Anne tore towards them, fuming.

'You should've stayed near your rooms!' she blurted. 'Why? For what joy – ?'

'Um, we were called?' offered Peter.

'For the love of God, Anne Ayon!' Edward yelled. 'What d'you expect? Our orders were to come to the Control Room! Besides, we didn't want to look like absolute dim-witted bastards just chilling by the door while an emergency was going on!' He said. 'Oh, and I did *not* run my wall down.'

'So *that's* what I heard in my room!'

'Shut up, Brer.'

'That could mean me, too.'

'Shut up, the *older* Brer.'

'Better.'

'All of you, shut up. Ugh, whatever. At least you're alive. We're running very late, and dare you do this once more,' she said angrily.

'Is that a threat?'

'Are you talking back to me, Toast?'

'Well, maybe I am! After all that has happened to me –'

'Shut up and get moving.'

They did. Anne took them down many different hallways, but finally, *finally* they made it to a bronze door. CONTROL ROOM, the silver sign on it said. Anne swiped a card against it. The door opened to a bitter Solseter frowning down upon them and the other Odyxenians yawning and sub-consciously drooling.

'About time,' Solseter said, his expression brightening. He clapped his hands as the other Odyxi jerked awake. 'Have some coffee if you want, everyone,' he said, pointing to a coffee machine nearby. Some hesitant Odyxi filled their glasses (which magically appeared every time one was taken, Edward noticed) and took a few slurps. He waited for them to finish, but Edward had the eerie feeling that Solseter was staring at him. If Edward had read his expression correctly, it said *I don't want any trouble. Be nice or be dead.* Edward decided to comply. Once the coffee drinkers were done, Solseter opened this arms wide. 'I'm terribly sorry to get you up at this hour,' he said. 'I know it's around two in the morning – I mean, we do have day/night simulation here, and I know two hours is a bad amount of sleep time. But we have an emergency I'm afraid. So let's get started.'

III

The Meeting

Solseter began. 'The emergency is far north, in Greenland. The Aurorans, a fierce alien tribe, have broken through the Earth's magnetic field and have crash-landed at Nuuk, the capital of Greenland. Their weapons are much more powerful than any man's. The mesosphere normally burns them up, and they are what we call shooting stars. Their ships, I mean. They have tried to enter the atmosphere for millions of years, but mostly failed.'

'So they nuked Nuuk?'

Solseter ignored him. Edward decided to shut up before Solseter made his head into a cannon ball to fight his archenemies.

'Sixty-six million years ago, their semi-successful entry still failed as they lost control of their ship. Earth's gravity pulled them down and it's rotation caused the ship to crash into the Yucatan Peninsula in Mexico. All their weapons blew up, causing many tsunamis and other disasters, almost wiping out all life on Earth.'

'Their target regions are mostly Greenland and Antarctica for it's safer to land there – the concentration of potential enemies are drastically lesser. Their spaceships' glow create the auroras that we see today. Yesterday, nine-thirty in the night, a spaceship has crash-landed near Nuuk. They were found by our Auroran Prevention and Extermination Society, or A.P.E.S. by Marie Samvan. As per our current data, the Aurorans have not engaged yet. Our job is to drive the Aurorans out *before* they launch their weapons. Any questions?'

Edward's hand shot up.

'Yes?'

'Mr. Solseter, how even are we supposed to get to Greenland from Britain?'

'My dear Odyxus,' (Edward got the feeling he was trying to play nice), 'we are not in Britain. We are on no specific place on Earth – we are in a place outside reality, outside space and time itself. The Portal in the Portal Room can take you absolutely anywhere you want through space and time. We are going to Greenland.' (As though the last part wasn't obvious. Sorry, Edward's mental status had already begun to wither.)

'Makes sense,' John said. 'Also, why are they called *APES*? Do they also look after primate welfare part-time?'

'John, can you think of a better mono-syllabic acronym for an extraterrestrial world-obliterator preventive pest-control force in less than five minutes?'

'Hey, I'm just saying *APES* just doesn't sound otherworldly enough.'

Solseter ignored him. 'Anyways, Anne, you're in charge, as usual. We need good gear. I will not be coming for I have a bit of time stuff to do – the Time Controller device is fluctuating; the Jewel's shine has diminished. I need to check what we've got ourselves into,' he concluded his lecture.

'Yes, sir,' Anne said. She opened her mouth to say something, but she never got to; a large *thud* interrupted her as a chair flew into Solseter. (No, it was not the loudspeaker this time. But both were equally annoying and deadly.) Odyxi gasped as they rushed to his aid. But Edward was looking in the opposite direction: he was looking at who caused it.

It was Paul. Paul Nium.

'Hey!' Anne protested; she had caught him red-handed too, and it's fair to say that no one escaped Anne Ayon. Anne unsheathed a sword – a golden hilted one. 'I never expected to use this on an Odyxus before,' she muttered.

Then she lunged at her opponent, but another Odyxus intercepted her mid-air, colliding with her, and they both tumbled down onto the floor. Edward gasped; it was Nick. Nick Evrithan.

But Nick's eyes were open, his mouth wide with shock. At first, it wasn't clear, but as Anne shored him onto the floor beside her, they saw the horrific scene: a rightful bloodbath, Nick's abdomen bleeding and Anne's legs cut horribly.

'You *bastard*,' Anne growled. 'Should've known better than to jump onto a sword.' As she held up her blood-soaked sword, there was a scream.

'Oi! where d'you think *you're* going?' yelled a voice. It was, unmistakably, Robin's.

IV

The Chase

Paul raced out the Control Room with the entire mob of Odyxi in hot pursuit. Anne led the furious horde through the labyrinth.

Paul raced through the labyrinth like a pro, as though he had been planning the entire thing for months. He scaled through the passageways as though they were no big deal.

Paul pushed open the heavy room door labelled PORTAL ROOM, which Edward remembered the quintets had passed by before on their failed mini quest of getting to the Control Room. By the time the Odyxi had caught up, they saw Paul disappearing through the purplish swirling Portal. Robin ran towards it, but by the time he realized it was going to disappear, he was too late – another head on collision with a cemented structure.

He'd run straight through the Portal Frame and hit the wall.

Edward's stomach turned; he knew this place. Then he realized: that was the room through which they had entered Odyxenia for the first time. As the thoughts flooded into his mind, he remembered the telescope, microscope and the other instruments. He realized that they'd walked through that very Portal Frame just a day ago, and that they hadn't noticed the Frame itself for they hadn't turned around.

As the angry party stormed back to the Control Room, they saw Solseter seated on a chair, rubbing this head. Edward had been so drowsy earlier that he just realized that there was a full array of electrical devices lining the room. 'Well, you're back!' he smiled. 'So, what happened?'

'Paul escaped through the Portal,' said Elsa, as Harry Pil, the medic-kid of Odyxenia, rushed over to Solseter and gave him some water. 'Thanks, Harry,' Solseter said.

'Mr. Solseter, I thought electrical things disrupted time?' asked Edward.

'Ah, that's a good question. These aren't electrical my boy – these are special computers fitted with non-rechargeable batteries. Batteries contain stored energy, so that's no problem. We get a constant supply of these things from our bases on Earth like those of the A.P.E.S..'

Edward was about to say something, but was interrupted by Anne.

'GUYS! Um, GUYS! Robin, stop juggling the computer mice! Ok, guys, listen,' said a bloodstained Anne. Edward realized she had been chasing Paul with her sword all this while, for he just noticed her sheathing it. 'We've got a *lot* of packing to do. And I mean it.'

'One second,' said Edward. 'Where's Nick?'

'Thought you'd ask. He ran off,' said Pil. 'No idea where. Maybe he took a detour to the Portal Room.'

'Um, so you mean Paul was distracting us while Nick readied the Portal?' asked Jack.

'Could be. The only other options are that either he still is in Odyxenia or maybe he left *after* Nium.'

'So if we'd just waited, we could've caught him?!' asked a frustrated Sam.

'Dunno. All we can do now is help with the mission. Usually, the A.P.E.S. handles it on its own, but if it isn't able to and it's calling *us* for help, then we've obviously got a big situation on our hands. Excuse me, but I've got some med things to pack.' And with that he ran off.

V

Packing for Greenland

While Anne got washed, all the other Odyxi began to pack. The quintets were busying themselves too.

Edward, Sam, Jack, John and Peter were standing in a circle outside their rooms (to which Elsa had generously guided them) and planned on what to bring.

'Swords are top priority if we're fighting,' said Edward.

'I'll get my bow and quiver too,' Peter said.

'Elsa did say that Ödyxenia is gonna supply rations, but I think the multi-nutrient bread is a good idea,' Jack added.

'Yeah, I think we should bring them,' Sam remarked. 'And the rest of the potions?'

'We'll give them to Anne. 'Cos we're using them only for emergencies, right? Better go with the emergency supplies.'

'Yeah, that works.'

'Oh, and, Ed?' said John.

'Yeah?'

'Seems like you and Solseter got along better already.'

Edward grunted. 'Shut up, Tern. Anyways, catch you guys back. I should probably go pack. And yes, I *am* trying to change the subject.'

And with that, they began packing and got ready for their adventure.

Sometime later, the loudspeaker came on. *'Everyone, report to the Great Hall, please. Edward, Jack, John, Sam and Peter are to take a left, right, fourth right, and the fourth door to your left. That'll take you to Robin's dorm. Robin, you are requested to stay back and escort them.'*

The quintets did as ordered, being careful to take the correct turns. There were only four, so they were relatively easy to remember. They reached Robin Dark's room in no time.

'Hey, Robin?' Jack called, knocking on the door. 'We're here!'

'Coming!' Robin called. The lock clicked as the door was yanked open by Robin, ready with a mini suitcase. He was dressed in a full-hand t-shirt and pants. He was also wearing gloves and a winter hat. His pale skin gave the impression of an overdressed hypothermic Inuit.

'Did you bring a microwave or something?' asked Sam as the quintets looked at the suitcase quizzically, wondering what on earth Robin was bringing. Robin answered, 'We're gonna have a lot to pack. There are also gonna be supplies in the Great Hall, so get some big bags.'

'But we don't have any!' Jack protested. 'We were peacefully playing tag when Solseter pulled us through the Portal!'

Robin thought for a minute. 'S'okay, I am pretty sure we'll have some extra handy,' he replicd.

'In the Hall?'

'Yeah.'

'Well then...'

'Let's get going,' Robin said. he led them down to the Great Hall. As they exited the labyrinth, they heaved the massive door open, and a crazy sight met their eyes.

'No *way*,' John said. 'Insane,' Edward remarked.

On the meeting table, there lay hundreds of stuff, like jackets, gloves, medicine and what not. 'Here,' Robin said. He leant next to a pile of huge bags, almost as big as his mini suitcase. 'Take as many as you need. We should have enough for everyone.'

They grabbed a bag each. 'I'll get you back to your rooms,' said Robin.

'Hey, thanks!' Peter exclaimed.

'Don't mention it. Meet me outside once you've *really* got everything.'

The quintets packed all the other stuff just waiting on the meeting table to be grabbed and packed and stuffed, and then Robin took them back to their rooms.

Once they were back out, bags full, Robin said, 'Guys, make sure you have gotten all you will need because we are not coming back until after the journey...if we're lucky, that is.'

VI

All Ready?

This time, the hall was teeming with jostling Odyxi, all carrying loads of stuff.

'Attention!' bellowed a sharp voice. The hustling and bustling in the hall ceased. Anne spoke up.

'Ok guys. I have this checklist with me for every single thing we need to take for the arduous journey ahead.' Anne raised a piece of paper in the air for everyone to see. 'Great timing,' Edward mused.

'Everything in the checklist is mandatory and is to be given maximum attention to while packing,' Anne continued. 'Understood?'

Everyone nodded. Anne looked at the checklist. 'Ok. Getting to the items...

'Jackets?'

'Yeah.'

'Weapons?'

'Yeah.'

'Gloves?'

'Yeah.'

'Caps?'

'Yeah.'

'Sleeping bags?'

'Yeah.' The yell was much quieter now, barely a whisper, but one could hear a lot of scuffling as many scrambled for the pile of sleeping bags on the meeting table.

Anne waited patiently. Then she started, droning on for several minutes, with multiple 'Yeah!'s being heard and occasional sneaking up to the piles.

'And lastly, matchboxes.'

'The *hell*?' erupted her audience. 'We might need to light emergency fires!' Anne protested. This time, every single Odyxi, even the seemingly overpacked Robin, tore towards the pile and snatched up matchboxes. 'Just make sure they don't catch fire. And with that –' she checked it off her list, folded her paper and pocketed it '– we are done with our list.' Everyone cheered.

Anne cleared her throat. 'And before we leave, I would like to introduce you all to one of our most valued A.P.E.S. members, the esteemed...Miss Marie Samvan!'

The door to the Great Hall slowly opened, as a beautiful girl emerged from it. Her hair was vanilla blonde, short and curled, and she was covered from head to toe with winter clothing. Even more than Robin, Edward noticed.

'*Bonjour*, my fellow Odyxi,' she said in a loud and clear voice. 'I am Marie Samvan from the A.P.E.S. in Greenland. I have just arrived here via Portal from the A.P.E.S. Headquarters at the North Pole, and that is where we'll be heading to now.'

There was a large round of applause.

'Well then,' said a deep voice. It was Solseter, who had arrived unnoticed through the open door. Most of the Odyxi jumped. 'That was a bit dramatic. And *very* annoying,' Edward muttered, jumping into Sam behind him. 'Agreeable,' Sam said frustratedly.

'Sorry 'bout that,' Solseter said apologetically. 'The Portal is still open, so y'all can go now. And good luck, don't get hurt, try not to die – and I wish you all *very* good luck with that – and please don't jump off a cliff! Listen to Anne to maximize your chances of living by the diameter of a bacterium. And please try to return, I need someone to help sweep the Great Hall.' He sounded dead serious. Anne didn't even protest.

Everyone groaned.

'Um, *merci*, Mr. Solseter,' Marie said, a little flustered and taken aback.

'And on that note, we're off!' Anne announced. Everyone marched through the corridors, and Solseter bade them goodbye as Edward stepped through the Portal for the second time in this life.

VII

The A.P.E.S. H.Q.

Just as before, Edward felt weird walking through the swirl. His vision blurred and cleared as the image of a room with instruments was replaced by a new one with an amazingly large hearth in its midst. There were four of them – one for each side – in the centre of the room. He also noticed many dispensers like hot chocolate and hot ice cream. (Was it *that* cold here you used ice cream to *warm up*? And how did they heat them up without melting them?) There was also an amazingly large water heater purely for drinking water.

As soon as they entered, they started to shiver. All except Marie. *'Portez tes vests!'* she said. 'Put on your jackets!'

This was followed amazingly quick. Caps, gloves, cloaks, boots, and more were hustled on. Marie said, 'Let's tour the place first, and then proceed further. Welcome to the Headquarters of the Auroran Prevention and Extermination Society, The North Pole!' The Odyxi applauded.

'How is it a team? Like, if you're the only one...' Peter said. 'Ah, the rest of the team is spread out over Greenland, my dear. I am in charge of satellite sightings and warning the other bases while the others report here. Here, there is nothing further North. This is the base at the North Pole connected to Greenland by the frozen sea. We express in distance to show where trouble is. So, yeah, that's 1660 miles south, Longitude 51° West, Greenland. More precisely, near Nuuk, the Capital of Greenland.

'Anyways, anyone wants hot chocolate?'

A noise like a fire truck siren combined with the 'peep, peep' sound of a clown's nose followed. Even Anne joined in. Everyone took a glass from a table nearby and poured themselves some warm liquid. Edward, amused at the sheer amount of hot chocolate still pouring into waiting cups, glanced up at the storage tank. It was almost as big as a bus, and it went through the ceiling to the next floor.

Later, they toured around the base with Marie. They explored the kitchens and bedrooms and computer rooms and radio-filled hallways and what not. Fortunately, the corridors were easy enough to navigate. The quintets heaved a huge sigh of relief.

'And here,' said Marie, 'is where you'll be staying.' She pushed open a heavy door. The floor was lined with...sleeping bags? The Odyxi spun around and looked at Anne, who was trying to pretend that nothing odd was happening, but failing miserably.

'You –'

'Anne!'

'You said –'

'Slee –'

'SHUT UP, EVERYONE!' Marie yelled.

Silence.

'What's the matter?' she asked. 'I asked them to pack sleeping bags,' Anne answered sheepishly. 'And –'

'These aren't *sleeping bags*!' Marie exclaimed, flabbergasted. 'They are storage sacks to store your stuff in!' she stared at the storage containers. 'See the lid-thingy?'

'Oh,' they muttered. 'Sorry, Anne.'

'S'okay,' Anne said. 'Hey, cheer up! We're off on our suicidal mission tomorrow!'

'*Tomorrow*?' Jack yelled with the same aghast expression the quintets had on their first voyage. 'Then why're we here *now*?'

'To arrange for weapons, food and other supplies, and so that you can get up early in the morning to get ready,' Marie replied. 'We could have directly gone to Capital Base, but now that the Aurorans are loose, they might intercept us there before we could get the warning. We decided to not take the risk. Now we have to make the journey there like any normal person.'

'Life truly sucks,' said Jack to his friends. The quintets agreed.

VIII

The Journey Begins...Sort Of

Early next morning, a loud yell on the radio woke them up.

'*HEY! COUCH POTATOES! RISE AND SHINE, SWINES!*' roared the loudspeaker. Then *Marie* yelled into the loudspeaker, '*SHUT UP, IGOR! Oh, sorry, folks, that was Igor Acko. He has –*' '*ADHD! AUTISM! MADDISM! I INVENTED THE LAST ONE, YOU KNOW, MY GENIUS –*' There was a slam and the loudspeaker broke off. They could hear Igor and Marie arguing in the Hall. Edward's ears rang. They gathered all their stuff and raced there.

'Ow,' Sam was saying, clutching his head as they made their way to the hall.

'Lemme guess, you ran into a wall?' Edward said.

'If you put it that way, yes. And I totally did not make a circular dent in the wall.' Edward began to wonder whether time distortion caused people to try to run through walls every time they get jump scared.

In the hall, Marie and Igor were still quarrelling. As Igor yelled something, Marie, 'Guys, *désolé* for this horrid introduction of –' 'WHY YOU TURN OFF THE RADIO!' Igor shouted. Anne stepped forward. 'Mr. Ackro, calm down! Please! You're making everyone paranoid!' But the boy paid no heed. 'TO YOUR ROOM!' Marie shrieked. Igor obeyed like a child; he took off the coat he was wearing and threw it on the ground. He then left through the corridors and was gone. 'AND IT'S *ACKO*!' his slowly diminishing voice screamed.

'Sorry for this uneventful introduction of my fellow mate and A.P.E.S. associate, Igor Acko. We shall start now,' said Marie sheepishly. 'I should've never let him on the radio.'

'Marie, do you think it's a good idea to leave Igor alone in charge of the base?' asked Edward.

'I'm sure he can manage. He only broke the projector and set fire to the dormitory rooms last time,' said she, her reply not at all convincing to Edward.

And with that, the Odyxi set themselves up for the mission. Marie had given the quintets some scabbards to sheath their swords, and Peter's quiver was hung over his shoulders, filled with golden arrows. His bow was also slung on his shoulder.

They all went to the area where the Portal was, and Edward realized the Portal Frame looked exactly like the one in Odyxenia. It was already lit, and they all stepped through the Portal Frame in twos after Marie and Anne, and Peter and Sam.

The arrival location was nothing like they had anticipated. There was almost zero snow around. Looking at their surprised faces, Marie said, 'We had to melt the snow around the Portal. There was danger of us freezing in time – literally. Though Solseter's Time Controller Device *could* potentially save us, we can't afford to put ourselves in front of such danger of half of our bodies here and the other half on the other side of the Earth...not inclusive of the fact that we're probably gonna die anyways, that is.'

They walked for a bit – only a few steps, mind – before Marie stopped them again. 'Wait,' she said. She walked a few steps forward and reached out her hand. Something solid obstructed her way. Everyone gasped - what was lurking there in *thin air*?

Suddenly, she *pushed* the invisible object away. 'This is an optical illusion,' she spoke to the dumbstruck Odyxi. 'The real Arctic is just outside this dome. It is there to protect the Portal from its wrath. Therefore, make sure you are wearing all of your protective garments.' She looked around. Everyone was already equipped. 'Oh, wonderful! Then let's go. Follow my footsteps, and don't hit the dome!' They did as told.

As soon as they stepped out, the terror of the Arctic came into view as they stepped foot into ankle-deep snow with the cold winds knifing through their cheeks. Just as Marie had asserted earlier, the Arctic was horribly cold. Marie took some long shotguns out her bag, and handed them to all the other bewildered Odyxi. 'We've been having a *little* too much trouble recently with polar bears,' she said as she passed them around. 'These just arrived this morning. We're heading to Capital Base now, the A.P.E.S. Base at Nuuk, and it'll be a long journey South. Follow me!'

Marie led them to a huge mountain of ice. Well, not on actual mountain, just a massive heap of snow, rather like a sand dune, but the complete opposite of it. Just at that very moment, Marie's watch beeped. 'Ugh, not another,' she grumbled. 'Not another what?' someone enquired. 'Blizzard,' she replied. 'Snowstorm.' The watch stopped beeping, now only a single, loud *PIIIIIIIINNNGGGGGG!* echoed through the desolate Arctic. 'These blizzards are pretty common, but they're a pain in the neck,' she grumbled. Seconds later, Edward began to hear rumbling, but the white infinity-room-like Arctic didn't help in actually revealing the malicious storm.

'BRACE YOURSELVES!' Marie bellowed over the noise of the approaching winds. In a swift motion, all the Odyxi, including Marie, were swept off their feet, and landed (unfortunately) face-first onto the snow (or at least Edward *assumed* they did). There were muffled squeals, but fortunately, the snow cushioned their impact. And they also got snow in their mouths – so much for oral reflexes.

'STAY PUT!' Marie screeched over the noise like a parakeet, even louder than Anne – high pitches worked well against low ones. The snowstorm blew harder still. Edward felt like he was going to get hypothermia (maybe he already did). His mouth was full of snow, and it *hurt*. Shameful to die well before the actual death game starts, he thought to himself.

Fortunately for the Odyxi, the blizzard slowly yet steadily came to a halt. Everyone pulled their faces out of the snow, shivering. Many had pink, swollen noses and cheeks, and some occasionally kept falling over dizzily. 'We're lucky,' Marie said, 'to experience such a rare storm. They last around three hours minimum – at least they need to, to be defined as a proper blizzard.'

She looked no different from the others. Edward could see bloodshot eyes. 'Back to the dome,' Marie said. They needed no more telling. They all went through the Portal and had a nice cup of hot chocolate before splashing their faces with lukewarm water.

Before they could set out, they heard footsteps above. Edward expected Igor Acko to fly at them, and once again start bragging horribly about his terrible word inventions and his disorders, and was about to suggest leaving *immediately*, when all of a sudden, a pale kid tore down with his backpack.

'*Justin!*' chorused the Odyxi. 'You're *always* late!'

'Sorry,' he said breathlessly. 'What did I miss?'

'Never mind,' Anne said. 'Let's just go.'

'FYI you just missed a snowstorm and a lot of pink noses,' Isa Persanne said.

Soon, they were back out, fortunately *before* they got the attention of the Headquarters' *other* resident.

37

IX

Winter Not~So~ Wonderland

They stepped out of the diorama dome for the second time, the chilly northern winds searing through their faces. 'Come 'ere,' Marie said, and led them to a shed behind the illusionary dome.

She pushed a button near its door, and immediately, the pulling of winches and creaking of gears could be heard as the door pulled up, revealing a large jeep.

'That's our ride to the Boreas Point,' Marie said, patting the jeep.

'Where's that?' Edward asked.

'That's what us Odyxi call Nuuk, the capital of Greenland. Nuuk just sounds too weird. And, well, that's where Capital Base is located, so...well, be prepared for the journey!'

As soon as Edward took a seat, he noticed many tiny buttons on the control panel. Marie followed his gaze. 'This ol' girl has everything we need. Icebreakers, heaters, auto-shooters; she even has cameras all around her. AI systems alert us of any danger,' she said.

'Damn,' he said, impressed.

Soon everybody took their seats. Seeing their bags on their laps, Marie pressed a button on the control panel, and immediately, a trunk on the back opened up. 'Toss 'em in there and sit comfortably,' she ordered. They did.

Noticing the shivering Odyxi, Marie activated seat heaters. Reluctantly, all of them agreed to start.

Marie hit another button. Suddenly, the engine coughed to life, and a steering wheel popped up. Edward heard some sounds at Marie's feet, and he assumed the accelerator and brake had emerged from their cover.

'Hit the pedal, Marie!' Anne yelled. Edward appreciated her perseverance – he could clearly feel the tension and strain in her voice. He didn't know how he himself sounded – probably much worse, not being a great optimist. Marie slammed her foot on the accelerator and their jeep shot forward like a torpedo, darting through the snow, shovelling heaps as it ploughed through them. Marie pulled a lever, and an icebreaker popped up in front. At the same time, the jeep transformed into a snowmobile. All while it was moving.

'Impressive,' Edward remarked.

He felt cold. Okay, *really* cold. The wind was slicing through his face. 'Temperature – negative twenty degrees centigrade,' Marie said. 'It'll take us around a day to reach Capital Base.'

'How're we supposed to sleep tonight, for God's sake?' Edward enquired.

'Don't worry; this snowmobile is an awesome convertible. She can even be transformed into a nice, big, wheel-less bus if required,' she replied.

After two tedious hours, Edward started to feel hungry. He reached into the trunk and pulled out his bag. He dug out his multi-nutrient bread. 'Bread, anyone?' he offered.

'Thanks, Ed,' Jack took one. 'Hey Anne! What've got for rations?'

'We've got, uhm, lemme see,' she pulled out a large bag from the trunk. 'Multi-nutrient bread, biscuits, fries, candy, burgers, more MNB...'

'What!?'

'Multi-nutrient bread.'

'Never mind. Should've guessed that.'

'And...a bunch of other stuff,' she said, zipping it close. She heaved it over her head and tossed it into the trunk.

THUD! said the jeep as both its trunk and Anne's bag collided under the force of gravity.

'One piece, please,' she said, pulling one out of Edward's packet. She then proceeded to pass bread to those in the front.

'Hmm, very energetic,' Marie remarked from the front. 'New variety,' Anne said. 'It's been what – six months, since you last visited? We developed this one pretty recently; it's taste's improved, and it also gives much more energy.'

'Nice,' said Marie.

It was a very arduous journey, not just for himself, but undoubtedly for everyone, Edward reasoned. The view didn't really improve too – just pieces of tundra vegetation sticking out here and there. Suddenly, Marie's voice nearly made him jump in his seat.

'We've not encountered any polar bears yet,' she said gravely and solemnly. 'They normally inhabit the area around here.'

Edward wasn't sure if that was a good thing or not.

X

The Cave

After the passing of a few hours, Marie pressed a button. Suddenly, the entire snowmobile shuddered, as chairs transformed into beds. The vehicle extended so that each bed took the length of the snowmobile's breadth, and everyone could rest comfortably in their own beds. Pillows and blankets automatically popped out, and Edward felt drowsy just looking at them.

'I'll call you tomorrow morning,' said Marie. 'We have to start our mission by noon.'

A tired Edward slumped on the pillow, and pulled up his thick blanket. Both were highly comfortable – this snowmobile must have cost a fortune! However, he couldn't sleep for a while; the trundling wheels, the cracking ice, the freezing wind and the clattering snowmobile made it nearly impossible. And just as he was about to close his eyes...

The snowmobile juddered to a halt. It started beeping. 'Fuel down,' Marie frowned solemnly. 'She won't make it no more. It's up to us now.' She climbed out of her seat. The others followed suit.

Edward rubbed his eyes. 'I barely sleep, like, ever,' he grumbled. 'And now, as soon as I close my eyes, the snowmobile stops.'

'Is he kidding?' asked Anne.

'Of course not! Did *anyone* sleep well tonight?'

'Yeah, thanks for asking,' Sam said. 'My head feels a lot better after that rest.'

'Well, good for you.'

'You, Edward Toast,' Marie said, turning to him, 'have slept for the last sixteen and a half hours.'

Edward looked at her. Marie didn't look like she was kidding.

'Well,' she said. 'We have another ten miles to walk. We should be done by the night. Get ready to trek.'

They clambered over to the trunk.

'Heave!' Marie said. They understood; they kept their fingers in the gap and pushed the heavy door upwards. The door creaked as it was lifted. Everyone pulled their stuff out. They then took their trekking gear out. 'Keep your weapons ready,' Marie said. 'There might be polar bears on the prowl.'

The shivering Odyxi shuffled through the endless snow. After a few miles of walking, Marie halted them. 'We camp here for the night,' she said. Edward scanned his surroundings. There was a small cave to their right, but nothing more. 'Who's volunteering to scout the inside of the cave to make sure it's safe?' Marie said, shooting her hand up before she was even done. Anne and Edward raised theirs, and a reluctant Peter followed them in, armed with Arachnis' bow.

'Do we *have* to scout the cave?' Edward asked.

'Well, if you didn't want to come, that would've been perfectly fine with me,' said Maric. 'But according to our exploration teams, this cave should have an exit. And if we successfully find it, our trek is shortened by over six miles –'

'I'm in,' Edward said hastily.

Marie lit a torch – the medieval kind, a long thick stick with a fire raging at the top – with the help of Edward's matchbox. They carefully stepped foot into the cave and made their way through, avoiding sharp icicles that fell occasionally. 'These icicles have lain undisturbed for thousands of years,' Marie said.

After the cave began to narrow, Marie took the lead, fire still billowing on the stick, followed by Anne and Edward with their swords unsheathed. Edward could see engravings on Anne's sword, but couldn't decipher it. Peter brought up the rear, armed with his bow, an arrow nocked, ready to strike.

Eventually, the cave opened up into a large area. The four Odyxi stood side by side. Marie smashed the icicles right above them with the torch, careful not to let the flames die. The fire was almost at her hands by then, so after breaking the perilous ice spikes, she chucked the torch down.

Edward made the mistake of looking down. He saw a huge chasm into which the torch fell, burning out as it made its long journey down. Horrified, he jumped back, cracking the ice below. 'Watch out!' Marie yelled, pulling them back. The tension in the ice settled, with a few pieces falling into the hungry chasm.

Suddenly, on the far end of the chasm, the icicles shook, fell and pierced the ice. 'Um, I didn't know the impact would travel *all* the way over there,'

Edward winced. 'No,' Marie agreed. 'It couldn't have. There is something else there that is disturbing the ice.'

Marie took out her grappling hook and shot it to the other end. The hook, whose job was to, well, hook onto the ice, merely hit it and bounced back into the chasm, dangling there. Marie retracted her line. 'The ice is too tough. We can't get over there.'

Suddenly, Peter's eyes lit up. 'Marie! Marie! I've got it! We're getting there as sure as my name is Peter! I've an idea!'

'What is it?' Marie asked.

'You'll see,' said Peter, smirking.

XI

Hello From The Other Side

Peter pulled back hard on his bow, the bowstring tensing, and nocked a golden arrow. He let go. The arrow smashed into the ice on the opposite side of the chasm at stunning speed, and almost buried itself completely. The only part visible was its rear end.

A smile crept on Marie's face. 'Are you thinking what I'm thinking?'

'Maybe I am!'

'Thinking what?' Edward asked, confused. Suddenly, Anne's eyes lit up. 'Peter Brer, you're a genius! Don't you see, Edward?'

'Erm...'

'Tie the ropes on the grappling hooks to my arrows. I'll shoot 'em one by one!' Peter exclaimed.

Without the torch, little light was now visible from the ceiling, no doubt being a thin layer of ice leading to the surface.

Edward smiled; the plan was getting to him. The four of them knelt down to untie the rope in their grappling hooks. Once they were done, Peter patiently helped tie them to his arrows. Bow in hand, he shot the arrows to the other side, one by one. Edward held the other end of Peter's rope for him. 'Everyone has the ends right?' Peter asked. His reverberating echo startled Edward, who let go of Peter's rope by accident.

'Oops!'

'S'okay. I'll go with you. But first,' he said, 'You must tie the other ends of the ropes to a few more arrows. I shall shoot them down here to secure them to the ground. Then, we can safely – well, probably safely – zipline over to the other side.' They did just that. Peter shot the arrows down with immense force to keep them steady. 'Alright, guys,' he said. 'Let's do this!'

'Um, Pete, are you sure that your arrows will hold our weights?'

'These arrows aren't regular ones, remember? They defeated a Dragon *and* a Giant. And you've faced a Giant yourself Ed – you *know* how strong they were.'

'Um, guys, we should probably get moving,' Anne said.

They performed the dangerous operation carefully. Peter stayed a little behind Edward for balance. Anne and Marie had clearly experienced such situations before, and were the first ones to reach the other side. They then helped the boys there. The four of them yanked the arrows out, and tugged those that were hooked on the cave entrance-side of the chasm.

At that moment, they heard a faint voice coming from the mouth of the cave, on the other side of the chasm. 'Marie? Anne? Edward? Peter? You guys there?'

'Hello! HELLO! We're safe!' Anne screeched, being a person known for a shrill voice.

'HELLO! ARE YOU GUYS FINE!'

YEAH!

'HELLO? GUYS! WE'RE COMING DOWN! DON'T WORRY! STAY PUT!'

Shoot.

'Uh-oh,' said Peter. 'I don't think this cave will take more stress.'

All was silent. But suddenly, they heard footsteps behind them, not from the other side of the ice chasm. Edward shivered, but was certain that it wasn't the cold this time. Marie yanked her gun off its holster and armed it. She bent on her knees and held it in level with her eye, facing the direction of the footsteps.

The footsteps grew louder and louder. The ice shook, intensifying the sound until they were so loud that they sounded like thunderclaps. Anne and Edward unsheathed their swords, while Peter nocked an arrow, ready to let go.

XII

The Encounter

ROAR!!!

The ice cracked. And out of the blue (rather, white) appeared something...white. It's footsteps echoed as the ice beneath their feet cracked.

It was a polar bear.

The bear lunged at Marie, who threw herself out of the way. The gun fell from her hands. Anne tried to stab at the bear, but the bear parried her strike with its paw.

'*Hell* no!' Peter bellowed, as Anne threw herself at the bear once again. She raised her sword and yelled, 'DIE!' but the bear threw her off. Marie unsheathed a sword and lunged at the bear once more, who dodged her, sending her skidding in the opposite direction. Edward started looking for an opening to shove his sword into the bear too. But before he could react, the bear grabbed him and threw him aside. Advice: Never get thrown into an icicle-infested wall by a 400-pound polar bear. It hurts.

However, Edward was quick to retaliate, drawing his sword at stunning speed, but no fault could be found with the bear, who dodged it and head-butted Edward. As he slipped and slid over the thin, slippery ice, he yelled – he was heading straight for the chasm! Peter quickly shot an arrow on the ice. It landed behind him, and he grabbed hold of it, inches away from the void.

Edward Toast was dangling over the chasm.

But before Peter could do anything more, the bear lunged at him too. Peter was small and quick, sidestepping with astonishing agility. The bear was now sprawled on the floor, as though doing a quadrupedal split. It now faced the same fate as Edward was, sliding and skidding towards the chasm – but with no one to help it. Marie and Anne ran up to Edward to help him. The bear was heading straight for the chasm – but straight at Edward! Clearly, the smart bear decided to use Edward to slow itself down and hopefully skid to a stop, and instead *Edward* would fall into the chasm.

It was flying butt-first into his face. Peter reacted quickly and created a sort of sideways monkey-bar staircase.

Edward safely climbed up, and flung himself out of the way just as the polar bear slipped past. The poor savage desperately hung on to Peter's arrows, but it's weight lead to its downfall. The arrow ripped off from the ice and the bear roared as it (and the arrow) tumbled into the chasm.

'Here,' Peter said, handing Edward's sword to him. 'It almost fell into the chasm.'

'Hey, thanks!' Edward replied. He turned around. 'Everyone okay?'

'Yeah,' Anne said. 'J-just a b-bit c-c-cold, but we're fine,' she added.

'Well, there goes an arrow,' Peter sighed.

'Peter, I thought you have, like, an infinite arrow supply?' Anne asked.

'I mean, yeah, I do, but still...'

Suddenly, there came the sound of ice cracking on their side of the cave. Only then did they take into account the wall in front of them.

It was made of extremely thin ice and there were cracks on it. One more *crack* got even *more* cracks on it. Then came a final *crash*, with which the ice completely collapsed. Behind it were two kids, laden with battle armour.

They looked familiar. And they wanted blood.

XIII

Behind the Ice

Nick Evrithan had made a full recovery after his rather gory bloodbath with Anne Ayon.

'You!' Anne exclaimed furiously. 'What on earth are you doing here?'

'Ah, we were about to ask you the same question,' Paul Nium answered gruffly. 'We just heard a battle outside. Frost's gone and you're all sweating in this weather.'

'Who's Frost?'

'Why, our pet polar bear of course! We heard a load roar slowly fading...'

'You killed him, didn't you?' Nick said, his voice quavering. There was a subtle silence for a few seconds. 'Anyways, why are you here?'

'We're here to teach some aliens a lesson,' Anne snarled.

'Ah, those Auro-thingies?'

'Uh-huh.'

'Well, if you're getting to our friends, you're gonna have to go through *us*.'

'*Friends*? For God's sake, what is *wrong* with you? Who in the whole wide world would befriend an alien?!'

'You've got a lot to learn, folks,' said Paul. 'Your knowledge of Time is limited to not much more than Odyxen and Solseter. Us? We have completed the puzzle. My advice? Join us. Learn the truth about Time. Otherwise, stop wasting ours.'

'Excuse me, but why this ambush?' enquired Edward.

'OK, well, we might've lied a little, but honestly, we knew you were coming,' Nick said. '"*Hey! Couch potatoes! Rise and shine, swines!*"' He mimicked the voice perfectly.

'No way,' Edward said incredulously. 'You mean – '

'Igor Acko's working with us, yes. And trust me, he has a big surprise planned for you guys,' Paul smiled wickedly.

'Now, hand over your weapons,' Nick said. 'Hands in the air, we'll let you go free. Or –'

'Or what, you blithering idiot?' Anne spat.

'Or you face the consequences,' he finished.

'We'll never back down!' Marie cried. 'We've a mission to accomplish. And *no one* gets in the way of the Odyxi.'

'We're Odyxi too, you know.'

'*Excuse* me?' said Marie, looking at Anne for an explanation.

'They broke out,' Anne answered her. 'Long story. Tell you back at Odyxenia.'

'Only if you make it back, that is,' laughed Paul.

'Well?' Nick said, tapping his foot on the floor.

'Well what?'

'Are you giving us your weapons or not?'

'No. I literally just said that we wouldn't back down.'

'Very well. Have it your way. Get ready for war.'

'Then battle it is.'

Anne drew her sword. So did Edward. Marie took out her gun, and Peter armed his bow.

They were ready for battle.

XIV

The Battle of The Odyxi

Anne charged first. She threw herself at Paul, but he dodged. He tried to snatch her sword, but she lunged at him, grabbing his ankles and sending him toppling. He countered by attempting a flying kick (while lying down) that made her release her grip. In seconds, they were back on their feet.

Meanwhile, Edward, being the only other short-ranged attacker, charged Nick. Marie and Peter covered him, shooting bullets and arrows that forced Nick to dodge them, keeping him on his feet at all times. Nick skilfully dribbled Edward and snatched his sword. He kept it by Edward's throat. 'Make any more moves, and he's dead,' he growled.

Peter carefully and stealthily drew out his sword. Edward saw him do it out of the corner of his eye, and Peter realized too. They winked at each other.

Peter waited for about three seconds. 'NOW!' he yelled. Edward ducked his head and punched Nick's armour in front of his abdomen. Fortunately, the reverberations and Edward's jump-scares aided him. His hand hurt horribly, but Nick's armour was dented. Marie took aim and shot, but Nick threw himself away at the nick of time, dropping Edward's sword. Edward took his chance, snatching the sword back, and hurtled it at Nick, who snatched Peter's instead. Nick dodged both that and an incoming Peter, and bolted away with Peter's sword, Peter at his heels. Marie shot a bullet, forcing Nick to duck. Nick Evrithan skidded on the ice, and a furious Peter snatched his sword back from the sprawled Nick on the ice. Nick immediately got to his feet and scampered away.

Now that their business with Nick was over, the trio turned their attention towards Anne Ayon and Paul Nium. Paul took every opportunity to attack Anne and dodge her sword. As soon as he saw the three advancing on him, companion run away, he took flight too in temporary surrender. The Odyxi paid no attention to where their foes had scampered away; they were too worn out to bother. Edward lifted the two swords as a symbol of victory, and handed Peter's to him.

They then heard a noise on the other side of the cave from where they had entered. The remaining

Odyxi had arrived. They looked at the four. The four looked at them.

Edward, Anne, Marie and Peter turned to look at the scene behind ice that had been brutally shattered to expose Nium and Evrithan. It certainly was their camp – there were two bunk beds, food, water and a bunch of other stuff that could last a team days.

'I think we should probably ransack this place for rations,' Anne said. 'Look – a door. That's bound to be the exit. Everyone got their bags?'

'Nope,' they said.

'Then get them, and ours too, if you may,' Anne said. 'We'll salvage whatever we can from here.'

This they did. Edward, Anne, Marie and Peter turned the place upside down. That was when Edward remembered something.

'Hey, Anne,' he said.

'Mmm?'

'What are those markings on your sword?'

'These?' Anne said, unsheathing her sword and pointing to them.

'Yeah.'

'It's Ancient Latin. It is one of the best swords ever made. It was made by Solseter himself. It reads D-R-A-C-O-C-C-I-S-O-R. *Dracoccisor.*'

'Dragon...' Edward scratched his head.

'Dragon Slayer,' Anne replied. 'It is the only weapon that can ultimately kill –' she stopped herself.

'Go on,' Edward prompted. 'Kill who?'

Anne sighed. 'I didn't want to break this to you Edward, but it's Sanguinarius – the Giant you fought on your first journey to find the Jewel of Time.'

'But he's already dead!' Edward exclaimed. 'He crumbled to dust!'

'Long ago,' Anne began, 'the children of Odyxen went to war. Always they fought with the Giants. The Giants, they realized, could only be killed with Dragon Slayer. At that time, only Solseter had the sword. But the king of the Giants, Sanguinarius, was already killed by his niece Tethys. Solseter gave this sword to me later when he began recruiting.'

'Once we had gained enough members, Solseter set to work with the Time Matrix. The Matrix allowed to travel through dimensions like yours by picking dimension doors at the Time Matrix Hall. In the end, we needed a quest to bring back the missing Time Controller Device. That's when you guys turned up.

'During the Siege, Sanguinarius – Sanguin – was there – back again. If only I had Dragon Slayer in my hand, I would've finished him once and for all. With the Jewel of Time, we can now track an attack on Odyxenia. At any given point, Solseter can use the *Matricontacters* to alert us if the Giants ever are back. We can control what is happening...in time,' she finished.

Edward listened intently. He remained silent, assimilating everything Anne had just said.

Meanwhile, Peter had gone to help the Odyxi on the other side. Everyone had now reached safely with the help of his arrows.

'We heard someone yell "Hell no!", and we got scared. So we decided to come down,' Robin explained.

Peter's face turned red as a tomato.

'Hey, wait a sec,' Edward said. 'Marie, haven't you ever been to Capital Base?'

'Of course I have,' Marie said. 'Why?'

'Then you would've known of this cave,' he replied.

'Ah, about the cave. Erm, actually, we had a different route earlier via an ice bridge, which collapsed soon after my last return. We got instructions from Capital Base to detour through the cave. Honestly, it's my first time here too,' she said. 'Anyways, let's go. It's getting really late.'

The weary Odyxi followed the direction Paul and Nick took to exit the cave. After they were out, the wind searing their faces, they got back to their journey.

XV

Capital Base

The entire party walked for seemingly endless hours, Marie in the lead. She kept shoving a long stick into the ice to check its stability and depth. Fortunately, they did take occasional refresher breaks to regain their energy every half-an-hour.

After a tediously long while, they managed to spot it – a large building sitting in the snow. It was hard to miss after miles of only snow and tundra vegetation. Behind the building lay a relatively calm...was that a village or a city?

'Welcome to Nuuk,' Marie smiled. The relief on everyone's faces was pure. Edward looked at the building. It was completely covered in black, with a large chimney at the top, making it look like an oversized cottage. But it looked much more modern, and it was quite big. There was only one thing that it could be...

Capital Base? Before Edward could say it out loud, Marie answered it for him. 'We're here!' she yelled. The others were positively jubilant, and with newfound energy, the Odyxi trudged briskly towards their destination. They walked up to a large, metal door, and Marie entered a passcode.

A small light on the door lit up. *'Waiting for authorization. Please stand by,'* an automated voice spoke. Soon, they could hear the clicks of locks behind the large door, and a young handsome teen opened the door and greeted them with a smile.

'Odyxi,' Marie said, 'Meet Thomas Tosausse, the A.P.E.S. operator from the Boreas Point!'

'Hey, everyone,' Thomas exclaimed. He shook their hands. 'Marie, urgent message: you can stay here 'til we build a new Headquarters,' he said.

'Um, *excuse* me?'

'You aren't aware?'

'Of what?'

'Oh Marie, I'm so sorry, but Igor Acko blew up the H.Q.! He sent us an audio recording – that your *friends* were going to tell you about it? I thought you'd know...I knew that guy would mess everything up! Trust him to take care of the base.'

Edward remembered now. *And trust me, he has a big surprise planned for you guys*, Paul had said.

'No,' Edward said.

'What do you mean, *monsieur*?'

'Acko is working for Nium and Evrithan.'

'Apologies. *Who*?'

'They are two rogue Odyxi who forsook Odyxenia and are now giving us trouble,' Anne explained. 'Paul Nium told us that Acko would have a big surprise planned for us.' Everyone listened intently. Just then did Edward remember that only the four who went into the cave actually knew about that.

'Oof,' Thomas said. 'On the bright side, well, come in everyone; I've got some nice warm hot chocolate waiting for y'all.'

The relieved Odyxi immediately removed their coats and relaxed in the warmth of the base.

'Hey Thomas, I've a question,' Edward said. 'Is this, like, the main base for the A.P.E.S.?'

'Erm, not exactly, Monsieur...'

'Toast.'

'Monsieur Toast. This is a branch of the A.P.E.S. – we are sort of like the defence system, as the Aurorans normally land around here and we are the ones who mostly take action,' Thomas replied.

'I see.'

'So,' Anne said, sipping her cup of hot chocolate. 'When are we starting?'

'Tomorrow,' he said. It's night.'

'Wait,' Peter said. 'I know it was getting dark, but not *that* dark!'

'It's the Arctic, *mon ami*,' Thomas replied. 'In summer, it never gets dark. However, there will be a slight shift in the brightness as you *are* pretty far away from the North Pole. But yeah, it will never be your usual night.

'There are sleeping bags in the rooms, you won't need yours,' Thomas said much to everyone's disappointment. Anne turned red this time. 'I will wake you all up in the morning. There are three rooms, pick whichever one you'd like.'

Edward decided to sleep with Sam, Peter, Jack, John, Robin. They chatted for a while before Edward became drowsy and slumped into deep sleep.

It seemed like seconds, but he was woken up by a loud 'GOOD MORNING!' over the radio. *Dang,* Edward mused to himself. *These Odyxenians were advanced* – how else would they have gotten radios to Greenland, let alone *two* bases? Maybe even more?

After Tosausse's rather frightening wake-up call, the boys changed quickly and torpedoed down to a large hall. In minutes, the others were downstairs.

Thomas entered the hall, followed by Anne and Marie who were steering a large table with wheels, laden with their breakfast - smoking bacon, toasted bread (no jokes please) and of course, the great drink of the Arctic –

'HOT CHOCOLATE!' Peter screamed. He charged at the cups, but Thomas cut him off. 'Calm down kid, we'll have these distributed in no time,' he reassured him.

In about five minutes, they were all seated in chairs (courtesy of Thomas) around the table, munching on their food while Thomas locked the wheels of the table and settled down for breakfast himself.

They quickly gobbled up everything *and* gulped down the hot chocolate in less than a few minutes. After a hearty, filling meal, the Odyxi helped clear away everything while Thomas explained their mission.

XVI

For Odyxenia!

He went to the front of the hall, where a whiteboard was placed on a stand. Thomas pulled out a marker pen from his pocket and began.

'Here we are,' he said, making a dot on the board. 'Here is the Auroran ship crash site,' he marked another point a few centimetres away.

'If you don't know the mission yet, let me explain. The Aurorans' spaceships, perceived by regular humans as asteroids, are aliens that have tried to enter our atmosphere many times in the past. Well, not all asteroids are Auroran spaceships, but some are. The mesosphere, the middle atmospheric layer, burns them up as they try to enter with their spaceships. They are seen as shooting stars. Meanwhile, their jet trail is most clearly visible near the poles as they find them easy entry points through the compressed atmospheric layers at the poles. Hence, there are higher concentrations of Auroran spaceships there. They circle the planet looking for possible entry spots.

'Very few have succeeded. The ship *Chicxulub* eliminated the dinos, for example. But they still succumbed to the Earth's defences. However, this time, we're certain that they've landed safely. All we know is that the Giant army is supporting them, so we might expect them anytime during the voyage and battle. Anne Ayon, you have Dragon Slayer, do you not?'

Anne lifted it. 'Of course I do.' There were a lot of *ooh*s and *aah*s, and others began to speak, but Thomas shushed them.

'The site is only a couple miles from here. Now that you guys arrived, we can start hunting the Aurorans down,' Thomas said. 'Now please pack your bags and come here. I wish us to leave by –' he consulted his watch. *Solar powered*, Edward read. What was up with these Odyxi? Why did they have solar-powered watches in such a cold and desolate place? How could they even work with no sunlight? Edward wondered.

'– five minutes,' Thomas said, jerking him back to reality. The Odyxi raced upstairs, grabbed their bags and flew down to find Thomas Tosausse fully packed, clutching a rifle with a scabbard around his hip containing a sheathed sword.

'Thomas, how do you think we can stop an entire superhuman fleet that has already wrecked the entire planet *sixty-five million* years ago?'

'We're the ones who are meant to stop them, Monsieur Toast. I don't feel highly optimistic, and I'm sure really none of us are, but –'

'Why don't we call in like the military or something?'

'Ah, because this mission...Odyxenia itself...you'd call it *confidential*. There are a lot of secrets that we definitely *don't* want to spill. Anyways, is everyone ready?'

'READY!'

'I've got my arrows and bow,' Peter said. Thomas acknowledged and heaved his own bag.

'For Odyxenia!'

'For Odyxenia!'

The Odyxenian troops stormed out of Capital Base and set out for battle.

The walk was slow, and the heavy bags didn't make life any easier for them.

After about a mile, Thomas called for rest. He seemed equally tired too.

After a few minutes (and munches on multivitamin-enriched Odyxenian bread), did they set off again.

In another half-an-hour, they reached the top of a massive hill, from where they saw it.

XVII

The Ship

On the massive valley spread beneath them, a gigantic ball lay. It was clearly made of metal, and was easily as wide as five buses put in a line. It towered over even the tall conifers of the Arctic, about three storeys high. And that was probably only a quarter or something of the gargantuan bowling weapon – the rest of it, God knows how much, lay buried under the thick ice.

But it was hard to describe owing to the state it was in. The ship's exterior frame was pretty cracked (though it was hard to make out from there), with numerous dents. Its battered surface made it look like a multi-gripping-holed bowling ball. It could have easily been the size of Nuuk owing to its highly enigmatic size.

Funny asteroid, Edward thought.

'Unsheathe your weapons,' Tosausse said. Edward, John, Jack, Sam and Anne wielded their swords, Peter armed his bow while the others loaded their guns.

'Remember, my friends. This is the last refuge spot. After this, there will be no backing out. I hope you are ready,' Tosausse said. Since no one answered, he crouched. 'The descent is steep,' he deduced. 'Crouch, like me, and slowly make your way down. But be careful - one wrong move and you'll be in heaven. And no more noise – I suspect they are still in that ugly monstrosity. Marie and I will take the lead. We will navigate the ice. Follow right behind us.'

With that, Marie made her way to the front and joined him. The Odyxi all crouched, and slowly trudged down the hill.

Fortunately, no major accidents happened. They slowly made their way down, one foot after the other.

Just as they neared the ground, Peter decided to use his arrow tactic to easily zipline towards the ground. They were low enough for Thomas and Marie to judge where the arrow should hit to prevent sinking, and Peter accurately shot one at the ground. A few arrows later, the Odyxi carefully made their way down. Peter came last, yanked the arrows out of the ground and tossed them back into his quiver.

They all stopped crouching. Thomas and Marie dropped their guiding sticks. All weapons armed, they shuffled forward.

It was only a few yards until the ship, but it took what seemed like an hour to get there. The Arctic did not help in judging the time.

Only until they were really close could Edward assess the giant ball. Tiny, shattered pieces of the ship on the ground could have easily fit a sleeping person on each of them. From here, the colossal metal spaceship seemed much bigger than it had been just a few minutes ago from the summit of the hill.

The Odyxi scouted the perimeter in an organised manner. They looked for possible entrances or traps around the ball, until eventually, Robin Dark yelled enthusiastically. (How? Gosh, these people had no fear of getting kidnapped by ambushing aliens who arrive in giant bowling balls that have trespassed all the Earth's defences.)

'GUYS! OVER HERE!'

They all rushed towards him. Once he was near, Thomas made him swear that he wouldn't scream again. 'Weapons up! They might ambush us,' he said. Edward took a moment to find the door. Finally, he located it.

It was also made of metal, and it camouflaged well with the surrounding ship. However, there was clearly no way to open it from the outside, he realized – there was no doorknob or anything. It had to be opened from the inside, but seemed to be slidable (though he didn't want to check that out). So of course Jack walked up to the door and tried to slide it open. But fortunately for the sake of Edward's sanity, Tosausse angrily pulled him back. After that, the Odyxi just stood there staring at it, clueless as to what they should do.

In a few minutes, suspense and nervousness built up in them. They were constantly shuffling around, when all of a sudden, they heard metal footsteps sounding like *clang, clang, clang* coming from inside. Swords raised, guns clocked and bow armed, the army of Odyxi stared at the door with anticipation.

XVIII

The Odyxi vs The Aurorans

The door slid open just as Edward had assumed. But he had not expected the horror that came from within.

It was green, pale as a cloud. In short, pale green. It had two eyes, with vertical pupils like a cat. It didn't blink, which just made the thing look terrifyingly like a doll. Eerie.

It had two arms and legs, and Edward judged it to be around six feet tall. It had an upside-down-pear-shaped head. It had neither a nose nor any ears, but holes on either side of its head and two antennae. (So *that* must be how they found the Earth – telecommunication signals!) It opened its mouth.

Edward closed his eyes and prayed he would be incinerated or sucked up into nothingness, but only a harmless chittering sound like that of a cricket's came out. Edward stared at it. It made another chittering noise and ran back into the ship.

'Let's try not to aggravate them,' Tosausse whispered to the huddled Odyxi. 'Don't shoot unless attacked. And *no noise whatsoever.*'

The alien came back, but not alone this time. It brought friends, and pinecone-like weapons that looked like they had just been yanked from a nearby Arctic pine tree. A large alien walked in front. He looked the same except he was a little taller and had a jewel stuck to his head.

Wait, what?

Was that...no, it couldn't be. Clearly, none of the other Odyxi had noticed.

The big Auroran chittered, and suddenly all the other aliens stood in attention, pinccones pointing straight up. Now it looked like he was surrounded by bodyguards. Then Edward speculated him to be their leader.

Thomas laid his gun down and raised his hands. 'We come in peace. Please, do not cremate our planet like last time. We respect you, King Grienfield.'

The King looked at them. 'We have, unfortunately for you, come to wreak havoc on your planet, mortal. Us immortal beings are way too powerful. Why, I oversaw the death of the dinosaurs! You will be a piece of cake. Even my bodyguards can confirm that the Chicxulub Mission was successful.'

Suddenly, John got a call from his *Matricontacter*. 'Matrix. John here,' he said. After a few seconds of creaks from the device, he put it back in his pocket and stared at the Auroran King with anger and astonishment. Clearly, the news was displeasing.

'Well, well, well,' the King boomed. 'Great news has arrived! Our allies are sieging Odyxenia –'

'Nium and Evrithan?' Edward yelled angrily.

'– again!' The King exclaimed.

Again? As far as Edward knew, there was only one attack on Odyxenia by Nium and Evrithan. Unless....

Anne's face darkened, proving him right.

Sanguinarius was back. Again. And this time only Solseter was there to defend the Time Controller Device.

Edward felt a rush of emotions: anger, sorrow, fear, disgust; all of them came pounding down like a ton of bricks.

But before he had the chance to say anything, Sam spoke up. 'I'm going,' he said. Before anybody could protest, he said, 'The fate of our existence lies there. No Odyxenia means no Portals, no return. Solseter's magic is the thin string keeping it from a bottomless pit. I'm going. I'm going to prove to you, King of Nothingness, that your futile attempts have no impact on us whatsoever. Your rule is worthless. Lose your dignity or lose your head. What do you pick? I suggest both. But pick fast – I don't have much time.'

Everybody stood speechless and stunned at his words. Then the King spoke, 'I am Grienfield, King of the Aurorans. If anyone dares to cross my limits, death will follow.'

'The Aurorans are nothing. They are inhuman, literally. They are compelled to obeying evil, not because of choice, but because of your exploitative powers. You are ruining them, Grienfield. I beg you, stop. Please,' Thomas argued for them.

'You've crossed my limits, Time Saviours. Now you shall face my wrath, and you'll be sorry you were ever born.'

He chittered, and not only did the bodyguards got into attack mode, but also more Aurorans poured out of the spaceship. 'Sam, go!' Edward yelled, bringing his sword down on an Auroran. It spewed black liquid and collapsed, but didn't crumble like the Giants. 'We'll hold them off!'

Sam took his cue and bounded up the hill

'May Odyxenia protect him,' Anne murmured.

'And wait! Sam, set *TIME* to *PRESENT* and *PLACE* to *ODYXENIA* on the computer!' Tosausse said. Sam shouted back what seemed like a reply, but he was too far to be heard.

Anne gripped her sword. 'Odyxi, CHARGE!'

XIX

Not~So~Epic Comeback

Sam

Sam reached the top of the hill and slid down the other side. Footprints were his only means of finding his way back. He hoped no blizzards would mess that up. Judging by his luck, well...he didn't want to think about it.

He travelled for a while. Fortunately, he'd ditched his heavy bag at the fight zone, and only carried with him his sword. He ran through snow's domain, and stopped to rest only when Capital Base came into view. Sam barely heard what Tosausse was saying, but he caught keywords like 'present', 'location', '......' and 'Odyxenia'. Well, he was hoping they were the keywords. He also heard 'computer' (maybe), but he had no idea how it was even mildly related.

After his short break, he tore into Capital Base and started searching frantically for the Portal Room. The problem? He hadn't the foggiest idea where it was as he'd never actually been there before. He just hoped he wasn't too late.

As doors flew open, Sam looked inside each room. He stopped at a room filled with computers, but later concluded that 'computer' wasn't referring to this. After some more looking, he found a door.

● PORTAL ROOM ●

He gave one good kick to the door, and it flew open, crashing into the wall beside it (oops). He looked around the room, finding many random stuff (other than the Portal Frame itself of course), but realized he had no idea how to actually light it, until eventually, he found something possibly of interest. 'Well, hello there!'

It was a computer. He figured it must be connected to the Portal somehow (as Tosausse said it, *probably*), but he had no idea how, or in what way.

With no other ideas, he turned the power button on. Instantly, it came to a screen like this:

He understood now. He changed *A.P.E.S. H.Q.* to *ODYXENIA*. Then he waited.

And he waited.

And he *still* waited.

Nothing happened. 'Noooooo...' he moaned and frantically started pressing keys on the computer. He finally gathered himself together. He *needed* to get there. And he would, no matter how hard it was. 'Hmm...' he said to himself. He pressed the "Enter" key.

It worked! Why had he been pressing every other key except that?

The Portal opened a swirly mass of thick purple, just as he remembered when he first stepped into it to get to the utterly bewildering, magical and twisted world of Odyxenia in the Time Vortex. He took a few steps back and broke into a run, straight into the Portal. Fortunately, the Portal teleported him just before he ran into the wall.

XX

Help Is Here!

Unfortunately, Sam had no idea why he did it, but it was done. His surroundings suddenly shifted to the Odyxenian Portal Room, but he was speeding headfirst into its door.

He couldn't stop himself in time.

CRASH!

'Owwwww!' he yelled and clutched his bruised head. Praying that he wouldn't get a concussion, he clutched his head and stumbled around the room.

Which had changed since the last time he'd seen it, actually. That was when they chased Nium and Evrithan. The time they'd left for the journey, he hadn't taken much note of the room.

The Odyxenian Portal Room was an unrightful *mess*. The instruments lay on the floor, shattered and broken; the walls had dents, as though they had been punched (or, quite possibly in fact, headbutted) multiple times; the door itself was on two hinges, with a few screws on the floor...the list was endless.

Sam sat down forlornly and observed the mess. He was too late, and he knew it. Now he was sitting there, head throbbing, while Odyxenia was being ripped apart with Solseter desperately protecting the Device, if not *dead*...

No. He couldn't be. He, Sam, would step up to save the day. Bearing the pain, he stumbled over to the door. He tried to open it, but it was locked. Bummer.

Wait, he was *stupid*! Of course the invaders locked the door, what was he thinking? They obviously didn't want any backup for the crumbling Vortex arriving. Sam judo-kicked the door, but still no. He thought and he thought, and he thought, and he thought.

He decided to take one last shot before...well, he'd probably give up. He unlit the Portal through the semi-intact computer, backed up into the now unlit Portal Frame, and pointed his sword directly in front of him. He took a deep breath and ran it down.

He only heard some splintering and rending of wood before crashing into the wall opposite to the room. Running was *not* his thing. This time, his head was saved but his arm took the impact. The sword punctured the wall and ran through it. He realized that the pain must be from when he smashed into the door, as the sword could only really make a cut in it, but if the door completely rent...it was his body. Definitely.

The next thing he heard were roars. And a yell. Sam rebooted his brain. He was supposed to be eating...no, not eating...oh yes, the fate of the entire universe depended on him not getting a concussion and also surviving and suppressing an attack by umpteen Giants who were well over twenty foot tall and had survived facing all the children of Odyxen combined multiple times over millennia. Great. Sam raced down the hallway, but not knowing the way, he had to rely on his hearing and hope that he wasn't heading straight to a dead end.

He ran up some stairs and down others, knowing he had to find it soon. Eventually, he came face to face with the door that said:

● GREAT HALL ●

Fortunately for him, he skidded to a stop right before he ran down his second door in five minutes. He tried it, quite certain that it'd be locked. It was.

This time, he rationally made a large rectangular cut on the door. He kicked the cut portion, and it sped across the hall, after which he heard a downright frightening roar. He knew that he'd successfully hit an invader (though he wasn't actually aiming to).

XXI

Saving Odyxenia

Sam Brer stepped into the room. This was too, just like the Portal Room, in a complete and utter mess. But staring at him from the other side was a large, bulky Giant with more by his sides. The only time Sam had seen these brutes was during the Siege.

'How are you here?' the Giant roared.

'What d'you mean?'

'I told him,' said a voice behind him. As the Giant scooted, Sam saw Solseter. He was quite unlike himself, however; he had a staff in his hand, and he had like, an *aura*, around him. Solseter had known that an invasion was about to come thanks to the Time Controller Device and had informed them beforehand.

Sam wasn't too late.

He raised his sword. 'I didn't want to miss all the fun,' he said. The Giant growled and grunted and roared and stomped, and he sent a minion forward.

Sam remembered him as the one who had tried to impede him from getting to the Shrine.

Sam, with no second thought, slew him instantly. A pile of dust greeted his feet. The King of the Giants ordered more of his troops to go forward, he himself duelling Solseter with...Sam didn't know what. He couldn't exactly see.

Sam ducked and dived, and slashed and slew. Piles of dust formed everywhere.

Solseter said, 'Don't let them gang upon you! Their unity is unbeatable!'

'Gang up on the kid!' the Giant bellowed at his men. Solseter gritted his teeth, fuming.

'Bruh,' said Sam.

'You shall fall to the unity of Sanguinarius' Giants!' the Giant King roared.

'Who's that?'

'Me, of course!'

He sliced through as many as he could, but the Giants were closing in. He dived through a Giant's feet, got up behind him and stabbed his back. The Giant groaned and collapsed into a heap of dust.

Sam took the other Giant by surprise. He sliced through them as they, startled, couldn't retaliate (or maybe they just had bad reflexes). Eventually, most of what remained in the room were heaps of dust.

A breathless Sam stood above them, triumphant. Sanguinarius was all on his own against a Son of Time and Sam.

'Now it's time for *my* minion!' Solseter laughed jokily. 'Go, Sam!' As Sanguinarius turned towards him, Solseter's staff released a sort of infernal heat blast, scorching Sanguinarius' backside. The Giant roared in pain and turned again, and was about to snatch the threatening staff when Sam ran through him, impairing him. He too, crumbled. 'Next time you come, remember to take some lessons on how to lock doors,' said Sam.

'That was daring,' Solseter remarked.

'What was?'

'Running at him like that.'

'Oh, *that*? It was nothing; I've had a *lot* of practice running through harder things.'

'Harder than *him*?'

'Clearly, he and his Giants tried to break the Portal Room door but failed miserably. But I, Sam Brer, have done the undoable. Oh, the wall too, by the way.'

'Oh, I see...wait *what*?!'

'Never mind. Anyways, I should've told Anne to come. She has that amazing sword of hers that can end these things once and for all.'

Solseter's staff dissolved in his hands and his aura disappeared. 'Sam, you are amazing. They will reform, but that is okay. Now, you must get back to your quest. And don't worry; this time, I shall join you too.'

XXII

Back to the Battle

Sam didn't fancy an old man accompanying him to fight, seeing as Solseter almost got himself killed, but his overpowered staff, aura and fighting skills changed his mind.

'They won't reform back in here? Like, in Odyxenia?'

'Nope. They reform outside, always. I've made it so that one can only use a Portal to get here. I hoped my defences on the Portal would stand, but, well...yeah. That happened. That's what Anne was working on back then.'

'In the Lab?'

'Yeah. She was testing out some new defences we were planning to use on the Matrix actually, but then you guys arrived and fixed everything, so we only need it on the Portal.'

The duo continued walking and eventually made it to the Portal Room. Sam apologised for the lack of a door. Fortunately, he was forgiven by the kind-hearted Solseter (Edward would have disagreed with that last part).

Solseter clicked on *CAPITAL BASE* on the computer and left *time* as *PRESENT*. He hit the "Enter" key. The Portal, fortunately, lit up. They stepped into the Portal together and arrived at the Capital Base Portal Room.

They walked outside Capital Base, Sam clutching his sword and hoping they wouldn't be late this time.

'How far is the crash site from here?' Solseter enquired.

'About hmm...half-an-hour, maybe?' Sam replied.

'WHAT?! We don't have that much time! Put your arms around my neck. We're flying.'

Sam was flabbergasted and abashed. It took him a while to assimilate the fact that Solseter could fly. As if he read his mind, Solseter said 'Of course I can fly! I'm a son of Time! I'm a god.'

A god who needed a ten-year-old to half-defeat his nemesis for him, Sam thought, but for the sake of getting to the battleground quickly, and not making Solseter mad, he decided against saying it.

He then awkwardly put this hands around Solseter's neck. 'Hold tight,' Solseter said. He started to levitate – like, literally, float two inches above the ground. As Solseter went higher, Sam felt it harder to hold on with gravity tugging at his feet. But as Solseter kept rising, Sam grew a little worried.

'How high are we going?'

'Only a hundred metres.'

'A HUN – !'

'Yeah. Not *super* high, but yeah, relatively high.'

Sam looked down. 'Don't look down. You'll lose grip,' said Solseter.

The ground was *pretty* far down.

'We must be, what, ninety metres?'

'Ninety? Ho, ho, ho,' Solseter laughed like Santa Claus. 'We're only about forty,' he said.

'WHAT!'

After that, no one really said a word. Sam spent most of his energy trying to cling on to Solseter, who spent most of *his* humming, not a care in the world as to how high he was going. But as Solseter started moving forward and picking up speed, the icy wind cut through Sam's face worse than ever. So much for speeding up.

'We should reach in about five minutes,' Solseter said. 'Let's get those Aurorans!'

XXIII

The War of the Arctic

Edward

If anyone was good at charging, it was Anne. She swung *Dracoccisor* and decapitated another bodyguard, then took to fighting the Auroran King.

Chaos reigned supreme as swords were swung and guns were fired rapidly at the enemy, but soon the Aurorans started bringing in catapults and cannons, and aimed straight at the battling Odyxi.

'Oh, we're *so* underprepared,' Thomas yelled, bringing his silver-hilted sword down and stabbing an Auroran in its belly. It collapsed, black blood oozing from it.

BOOM! BOOM! BOOM!

Cannons fired as Odyxi scattered. The King Grienfield knocked Anne backwards, and Tosausse and Samvan, both raising their silver-hilts, rushed in to parry another swing.

In seconds, Anne was up again, charging the King of the Aurorans, but so were the catapults.

Massive rocks hurtled at amazing speed at the Odyxi. The Aurorans ducked to avoid getting hit by the boulders, but the startled Odyxi were forced to blast them with their guns or slice them with their swords (in which case two halves rolled on either side of them). Edward desperately wished he'd brought his laser guns from their last adventure.

The Odyxi were getting pushed back by the many arriving Aurorans to the point where Edward began to wonder, even though its sheer size, how all those Aurorans could possibly fit in that ship.

And it wasn't just Aurorans who came out – almost every Auroran was carrying a weapon, from swords and guns to more armed cannons and catapults and other complex high-tech machinery and weapons that no one could comprehend.

At that point, it seemed only long-ranged weapons would be effective, so the sword-wielders grabbed their own guns and started firing, using the rocky terrain for cover. They hid behind taller rocks to reload their guns. Anne, who didn't have her own gun, took Sam's. They took every chance they got to take a shot at the enemy.

Unfortunately, the Auroran ship's crash made sure that not many jutting-out things remained, and hence they were heavily deprived of rock cover. The catapults didn't help, destroying much of the remaining regions that helped the Odyxi take cover.

However, slowly yet surely, the Odyxi regained their ground as their (the Aurorans') numbers depleted. With one final push, the entire fleet of Odyxi charged out of their temporary hiding spots and at the Aurorans.

Edward occasionally snuck up behind an Auroran and stabbed it, disgusting black blood spewing all over him. Eventually, only the Auroran King Grienfield remained.

The King yelled and tried to swat at Edward, but Edward parried the strike with his own sword. At that point, he didn't expect things to possibly get any crazier.

Imagine his surprise when he saw two figures flying above the hill which they'd descended not very long ago.

XXIV

The Battle Concludes

Sam Brer and Solseter descended, literally, in the middle of the battlefield. Before Edward could even notice the landing, the King knocked him down and he passed out.

Well, not completely.

He could still hear yells, screams, bangs and other noises one might hear during a battle.

Suddenly, he was jolted awake by a huge splash of water on his face.

Elsa looked down on him. 'Well, there goes the water bottle,' she said.

'Wait, you used your bottle to save me? Thank you!'

'No, idiot. Yours.'

She left him looking dumbfounded (and soaking wet).

Edward got up, and the first thing he noticed was that the Aurorans were gone. In their places were dozens, if not hundreds of dead bodies with black pools of blood surrounding them. There must have been more Aurorans teeming out of the ship, as he didn't remember seeing *these* many dead alien bodies. And when he passed out, only Grienfield had remained.

The next thing he saw was the Odyxi surrounding something. The grunts sounded like it was Grienfield. As he made his way into the crowd, he saw the scene: Solseter standing over the Auroran King with his staff raised, Anne's sword raised over the King's head. Peter held his bow, an arrow ready to strike the King.

'Only *Dracoccisor* can destroy me,' he cackled. 'Neither your staff Solseter, nor your bow, child, can end me. And of course, never a simple sword.'

'No, Grienfield. You have understood wrong. The staff and bow are to keep you in check. If shot at the leg, the arrow cannot turn you to dust. And the sword? That *is* Dragon Slayer,' Solseter said. 'Anne, show him.'

Anne sneered, showing him the carved name on her sword. Grienfield started gasping.

'Before we kill you, Grienfield, we have something to tell you,' said Thomas, stepping out from the crowd. 'The Giant Army has failed once again. The Time Controller Device is safe. I've worked for over three months as an A.P.E.S. member, but never before have I felt such success in my life. And today – '

'SHUT UP!'

'*Hem hem.* As I was saying – '

'I said, SHUT UP!'

He tried to wriggle free of something, but Solseter held his staff high. 'Escaping isn't allowed, my friend. The A.P.E.S. have won over you. Accept your defeat. You will now be slain for good. The Giant Army shall never prevail.'

With that Anne swung her sword, however Solseter clearly accidentally eased his control over the Auroran. The Auroran smashed his fist into the sword, which due to its powerful magic, stayed intact. He raised and pulled his legs back, ready to bring them down on Peter, but the panicked Odyxus inadvertently shot an arrow at the King, who collapsed in a heap of dust.

The Auroran king was gone. And he would be back.

XXV

A Triumphant Victory

'Aren't there more though?' Edward asked.

The Odyxi had begun their long walk back towards Capital Base, and Edward gingerly held the liberated Jewel of Time in his hands. Grienfield's head had safely deposited it in the snow.

'There will be, on their planet, yes,' Anne said. 'But hopefully, they wouldn't return yet. The journey is very long and arduous, and they need a lot of provisions and fuel to make it. As said before, the last trip they made to Earth was over sixty-five million years ago, when the dinosaurs went extinct. Then, the ship's crew died owing to the explosion, so this time I think Grienfield decided on a softer landing. Way too soft. Otherwise we'd have been blown up into smithereens if we'd ever left Odyxenia – there would be no Earth left to go to. Only the Vortex would have protected us,' she ended.

Meanwhile, Peter Brer looked like on the verge of tears. He kept apologising again and again for the incomplete death of the Auroran king. Everyone else was trying to calm him down.

The rest of the walk was pretty tiring, but Sam told them his story which made time go by a little quicker. When he came to the part about Anne's disappearance during the feast, everyone stared at Solseter and Anne. But Anne didn't even protest; everyone was in a jubilant mood, grinning and talking and laughing together. Edward smiled to himself – he had successfully made it through two challenging adventures.

Solseter, however was very exhausted from the fight in Odyxenia, carrying Sam to the battlefield and especially controlling Grienfield. So, they had to walk.

But the trek was definitely less time-consuming as they were all in a triumphant mood. Anne was particularly interested about Sanguinarius' rather incomplete death. 'He will reform again,' said Anne. 'It could be hours, days or even months. But only after he is fully dead, can we complete our mission as the Odyxi. Only then will the purpose of Odyxenia be fulfilled and we return to Earth victorious.'

Soon, they were all at Capital Base and they sauntered towards their rooms. One by one, they all washed themselves and changed into brand new clothes stashed at the base.

Alas, it was time to say goodbye.

Edward shook hands with Thomas and Marie. 'Until we meet again,' he said. Thomas grinned. Solseter promised them that he would see to the reconstruction of the A.P.E.S. H.Q., and he also requested Samvan and Tosausse to keep him updated about any Aurorans.

They walked to the Portal Room of Capital Base. Solseter stepped through first. He disappeared through the purple Portal.

Edward waited for someone to step in, when, from behind him, Anne said, 'You first, Edward.'

He walked to the front of the newly lit Portal. He put one leg through the Frame, then the next.

XXVI

The Vision

Edward had arrived...somewhere. But he knew he wasn't at Odyxenia.

He had no idea when, where, how and why he arrived there. He started to observe his eerily peaceful surroundings.

He had teleported to a foggy land, so foggy that nothing was seen apart from it. He stepped through the fog.

The fog reminded him of the mist that hid the door of the Matrix. And just like he did then, he felt his way towards the end of the fog.

As he stepped out of it, a terrifying sight met his eyes: a massive whirlpool swirling around in a huge sea with a woman, wearing bright blue, tied to a rock right beneath it.

She looked beautiful; but her eyes were full of sadness. Edward's head nagged with questions. Who was she? Where was she? Was she alive? When did she get here? What had happened to her?

Edward was at the bottom of the ocean, but he could breathe and even swim. The pressure didn't blow him up. He barely even felt wet, if ever.

He walked over to the woman. Yes, walked, not swam. He didn't understand how – he could get into a moving coaster, but couldn't swim like normal, drown, or even run out of air.

Suddenly, she tilted her head and stared at him. Edward was literally taken aback.

'Um...hello, I'm Edward. Edward Toast,' he said uneasily. Of course, just like in the Matrix, Edward thought she wouldn't be able to hear him. But to his surprise, she spoke to him.

'Hail, Toast. It hath been thousand years since I was lost. At the last, I have found one with whom to speak.'

'Wait, how ol-?'

'That is naught of import. Tell thy master that I am trapped here. This be but a vision – thou canst speak with me.' (As though she read his mind). 'Mine powers are weak. Tell him. Go forth. Anon.'

'Wait –'

'Nay! Go! The vision shall perish with thee within it. Run! I beg thee!'

Edward ran face first into the fog. He didn't know who she was, or why she was talking in that crazy Shakespearean dialect. Anyways, he tore towards the end of the mist and found a door. He jumped in just as he heard noises of self-destruction and arrived...

XXVII

The Queen Of Seas

Back at Capital Base.

Everyone was still there. 'What happened?' asked Sam. 'You okay, man?'

As over twenty eyes settled on him intently, he said, 'I'll tell you back at Odyxenia.'

He took a deep breath and stepped into the Portal once more, but this time, fortunately, he ended up back at the Odyxenian Portal Room where Solseter was waiting.

One by one, the remaining Odyxi arrived. Eventually, they made their way to the Great Dining Hall, where platters of food were laid out on the tables.

Edward ate hungrily, gobbling his food. Once they were done with dessert (amazing choco-vanilla cake), they all – including Solseter – sat listening to Edward.

'So, Edward,' Solseter said calmly. 'Anne here told me you took a...ah, detour,' he added. 'Would you please –'

'Okay, okay, I am,' Edward said.

'Take your time,' said Anne kindly, clearly sensing his frustration. 'You can – '

'CAN YOU STOP!' Edward yelled, suddenly standing up. Everyone jumped, aghast.

'I'm sorry. It's just...traumatizing. I will explain.' He sat back down.

'So there was this misty thing...like you know, as in the Matrix...but, like, I could communicate with people.'

He took a deep breath. 'Go on,' Solseter prompted him.

'I was under the ocean,' he said, more steadily this time. 'Then there was this really beautiful lady in blue robes and chained to this massive rock...she said she was super old and...I had to tell my "master", I presume Solseter, that she's stuck. She didn't mention details, but...yeah, she's in trouble. And she kept talking in Shakespearean English. I think she used her power to create the vision...and she was clearly super weak. I could feel it – the vision – self-destructing behind me. I ran back to the door...and...yeah.'

They were all quiet for a long time. Edward took his first calm moments of processing this information.

'So...she was in full blue, you say,' said Solseter slowly.

'Uh-huh.'

'And she could breathe under the ocean.'

'Well, clearly, *she* was *there* and only I was in the vision, so yeah. But I could too.'

'And how old was she?'

'She said she hasn't spoken to anyone in thousands of years. At least I *think* that's what she said. So she's definitely much older than that. My guess is that she is immortal if she can live that long or maybe just super powerful. Or both.'

Solseter rose. Everyone held their breath, waiting for him to say something.

'It is her,' he said finally, with an air of authority and mirth.

'Oh my goodness, *no way*!' yelled John. 'It is *her*!'

'Shut up, Diss,' said someone.

'Well mister, who is it?' asked Edward.

'My niece Tethys. The Goddess of the Seas.'

XXVIII

The New Mission

'You have a *niece*?' exclaimed Sam. The entire hall suddenly erupted in a frenzied commotion.

'Yes.'

After a long time, things slowly started to settle. They all sat down. 'So,' said John. 'She's the mission?'

'Well, even I didn't expect her to still be alive after so many years. She might have some clues as to where the others are though. I think its best if we go after her.'

'The *others*?'

'Odyxen has a big family tree.'

'Oh.'

'Come,' Solseter said. He led the party through the labyrinth to the Control Room. 'The first thing to do is to figure out her location,' said he. 'But I've got that covered.'

He typed something on the computer and immediately a pulsing dot appeared on a world map. 'We thought she was dead, so we never used this.'

'*You* thought she was dead,' Robin corrected him.

'Well...I suppose so. Looks like...somewhere near Miami,' he said, looking at the map.

'My...if it's not –'Anne began

'The Sea of Monsters.'

Silence. 'Um, excuse me, but we arrived, like, three days ago,' Edward said angrily.

Anne stood up. 'The Sea of Monsters, better known by humans as the Bermuda Triangle, connects the cities Bermuda, Miami and Puerto Rico. It was once the prison of Tethys, but captive sea monsters escaped a couple million years ago and no one, absolutely *no one* could stop them. Regular humans don't ever know the cause of disappearing ship and planes.'

'Why would Tethys be in her own prison?'

'The monsters that escaped. They trapped her. Or at least...well...it's a good guess to start with.'

'Do we have any kind of lead on them? Like actual proper leads, not speculatory ones,' Sam asked Solseter.

'Lemme check my computer...'

'Anything?' Sam asked after a while of Solseter *click-tick-tap-clacking* on it.

'Nope,' he said, revolving his chair to face the Odyxi. 'Well, I might know a few things about the monsters though.

'The largest monster is of the species *Architeuthis gargantulus –*'

' – which probably doesn't exist –'

' – which humans know better as the Kraken. It is a massive squid slash octopus reaching a hundred feet or thirty metres in height. And that's just the first.'

'Of what?'

'Of all the monsters in the long list that are currently guarding the Queen of the Seas. Here's the next.

'You see, a few million years ago, Tethys led her armies against the Megalodon – the *Otodus megalodon –* and had had it captured. This ferocious shark is about half the size of the Kraken and almost equally deadly. The Kraken, like any other squid, uses suckers to grab onto its prey. But the Meg is an extremely agile creature unlike its counterpart, and has sharp teeth measuring nearly five inches in length. It has an extremely strong bite force enough to crush even an armoured dinosaur into smithereens.'

'There are also a few other sea creatures I don't know much about – a *Plesiosaurus*, a giant sea scorpion called *Jaekelopterus* and some more. Others like the Loch Ness Monster – the *Nessiteras rhombopteryx* – and the Leviathan – the *Serpentes livyatanus* – live in other regions like the Loch Ness and the Mediterranean. But that is, unfortunately, everything I know about the Sea Prison of Monsters.'

The Odyxi sat pondering about this. These muscular beings were way stronger than them, and they completely outmatched in strength. Why, the Aurorans had almost destroyed, pummelled and smote them. Okay, the Aurorans had powerful weapons, but Edward didn't delight in the advent of the prospect of an Odyxi sandwich.

'You know what,' said Anne. 'I might just make something like that...'

'You're making a Meg and a Kraken?' asked Edward.

'Wait and watch,' Anne smirked.

THE TIME GLOSSARY

Arachania: The new Queen of Arthropods and successor of sister Arachnis.

Arachnis: The former Queen of Arthropods and predecessor of sister Arachania slain by Peter Brer.

Arachnis' Bow: The golden bow (and arrows) of Arachnis who had given it to Peter Brer in her dying breath.

Auroran: An alien under the rule of Grienfield set on destroying the world.

The A.P.E.S. (The Auroran Prevention and Extermination Society): A team of Odyxi stationed in Greenland and the North Pole that track and update Odyxenia about the Aurorans.

The A.P.E.S. Headquarters: The A.P.E.S. Base located at the North Pole, in charge of warning other A.P.E.S. bases of any Auroran sightings in the sky, headed by Marie Samvan.

Boreas Point: The Odyxenian name for Nuuk, the Capital of Greenland, where Capital Base is located.

Capital Base: The A.P.E.S. Base located at Nuuk (Boreas Point), the Capital of Greenland, that is the primary attack station of the A.P.E.S. and headed by Thomas Tosausse.

Chicxulub: A crater formed by the asteroid Chicxulub Impactor sixty-six million years ago that was one of reasons for the extinction of the dinosaurs. **(Here):** The mission/ship guided by Auroran King Grienfield that saw to the death of the dinosaurs.

Dracoccisor: Anne Ayon's golden-hilted sword, 'Dragon Slayer' in Latin, made by Solseter, that is the only sword that could completely vanquish any enemy and prevent them from reforming.

Grienfield: The immortal king of the alien tribe of Aurorans who oversaw the Chicxulub Mission.

Jewel of Time: The component of the Time Controller Device retrieved by Edward Toast from the Time Matrix that detects any enemies trying to enter Odyxenia by fluctuating.

Odyxen: The God of Time.

Odyxenia: A Time Base in a reality outside time and space that houses the Odyxi.

Odyxenian: A member of the Time Base of Odyxenia; relating to Odyxenia.

Odyx(us)(i): The member(s) of the Time Base of Odyxenia who go on missions to save Time.

Portal Frame: The metal frame around a Time Portal.

Solseter: A son of Odyxen who created Odyxenia and recruited the Odyxi.

Tethys: The Goddess of the Seas, granddaughter of Odyxen and niece of Solseter.

Time Controller Device: The device assembled through different parts retrieved from the Time Matrix by Edward Toast, Sam Brer, Peter Brer, Jack Olan Tern and John Diss including the Jewel, the Shrine, the Key, the Slot and the Volter that help activate the Jewel. It detects any enemies trying to enter Odyxenia through the fluctuations of the Jewel.

Time Matrix: The inter-dimensional reality that allowed secret unsensed passing used by Odyxi to retrieve items lost in Time.

Time Vortex: The reality outside time and space where the Time base of Odyxenia is located.